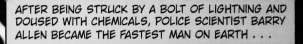

AFTER BEING STRUCK BY A BOLT OF LIGHTNING AND
DOUSED WITH CHEMICALS, POLICE SCIENTIST BARRY
ALLEN BECAME THE FASTEST MAN ON EARTH . . .

SUPER DC HEROES

THE FLASH

WRITTEN BY
JANE MASON

ILLUSTRATED BY
DAN SCHOENING,
MIKE DeCARLO, AND
LEE LOUGHRIDGE

CAPTAIN COLD'S
ARCTIC
ERUPTION

STONE ARCH BOOKS
a capstone imprint

Published by Stone Arch Books in 2011
A Capstone Imprint
151 Good Counsel Drive, P.O. Box 669
Mankato, Minnesota 56002
www.capstonepub.com

Library of Congress Cataloging-in-Publication Data
Mason, Jane B.
  Captain Cold's arctic eruption / written by Jane B. Mason ; illustrated by Dan
Schoening, Mike DeCarlo, and Lee Loughridge.
    p. cm. -- (DC super heroes. The Flash)
  ISBN 978-1-4342-2617-4 (library binding) -- ISBN 978-1-4342-3089-8 (pbk.)
  1. Graphic novels. [1. Graphic novels. 2. Superheroes--Fiction.] I. Schoening,
Dan, ill. II. De Carlo, Mike, ill. III. Loughridge, Lee, ill. IV. Title.
  PZ7.7.M377Cap 2011   2010025593

Summary: Within hours, a monstrous volcano will destroy a Pacific island and
all of its citizens. The Flash has done everything he can, but there's only one
way to stop the disaster . . . cool the volcano's magma chamber. Unfortunately,
only one man is capable of such a task . . . his archenemy, Captain Cold. The
Scarlet Speedster cuts a deal with this frosty felon, and they're off to save the
day. But Captain Cold cannot be trusted. While firing his freeze gun into the
volcano, this sneaky super-villain sees an opportunity. He'll turn the tropical
paradise into his personal tundra.

Art Director: Bob Lentz
Designer: Brann Garvey
Production Specialist: Michelle Biedscheid

Printed in the United States of America in Stevens Point, Wisconsin.
092010
005934WZS11

TABLE of CONTENTS

MEGA-ERUPTION

Barry Allen frowned as he watched the evening news. The scene on the screen was beautiful, showing a brilliant tropical landscape. The Pacific Ocean sparkled in the sunlight, and white-capped waves lapped at the golden sands.

Mount Lavalo, the biggest mountain on the island of Wiji, stood tall against a clear blue sky. It was lovely to look at. But Barry, who was secretly the Flash, was not concerned with how Mount Lavalo looked. He was concerned with how it was acting.

"A number of recent earthquakes in the South Pacific have scientists worried," said the news reporter on TV. "According to geologists, a mega-eruption on Mount Lavalo is coming soon. Although dormant for 83 years, strong evidence suggests that this could be the biggest and most lethal eruption Wiji has ever seen."

Barry groaned. He knew that mega-eruptions could destroy half a continent with their boiling lava. And, even worse, their ash could block the sun for months.

"Homes and businesses are being evacuated," the news reporter continued. "But, if predictions are true, no amount of preparation can help this doomed nation."

The TV screen flashed to several historic volcanic eruptions. In each case, the skies were blackened by tons of gray ash.

None of these eruptions were mega-eruptions. Human beings had never witnessed one before — this would be the first in 30,000 years.

As the Flash, Barry Allen was blindingly fast and capable of incredible feats. But when it came to a mega-eruption, the Flash was in over his head. He could do a lot of things, but he couldn't prevent the biggest volcanic eruption in history — not by himself, anyway.

"The only way to stop the eruption is to cool the magma chamber," a scientist on the TV told the reporter. "But that's impossible. It would require an enormous amount of refrigeration in order to lower the temperature of the super-heated heart of the volcano."

"Impossible?" Barry repeated.

The World's Fastest Man was sure that cooling this pool of molten rock beneath this volcano was possible. In fact, he knew one person who could handle the task.

"But *would* he?" Barry said aloud. He didn't like the idea that was creeping into his brain. How could he team up with his archenemy? How could he join forces with a super-villain?

"This island could disappear under a heap of molten lava forever," said the TV reporter.

Barry Allen sighed. An entire nation was in grave danger, and he could think of only one way to help. "I have no choice."

Captain Cold had recently been released from prison. The conditions of his parole were strict.

His parole required him to make his location known to police at all times. Since Barry was a police scientist, finding the criminal's cell phone number wasn't hard.

"I'm busy!" Captain Cold shouted into the phone. "What do you want?"

On the other end of the line, Flash closed his eyes and gritted his teeth. This was the last thing he wanted to say. "Your help," he admitted quietly.

HAHAHAHA! Captain Cold laughed like an Arctic wolf. "Oh, Flash, you puny speedster," he said. "I knew you'd come calling. But what makes you desperate enough to ask for my help?"

"A volcano," Flash explained, trying to keep himself cool. "The biggest eruption the world has ever seen."

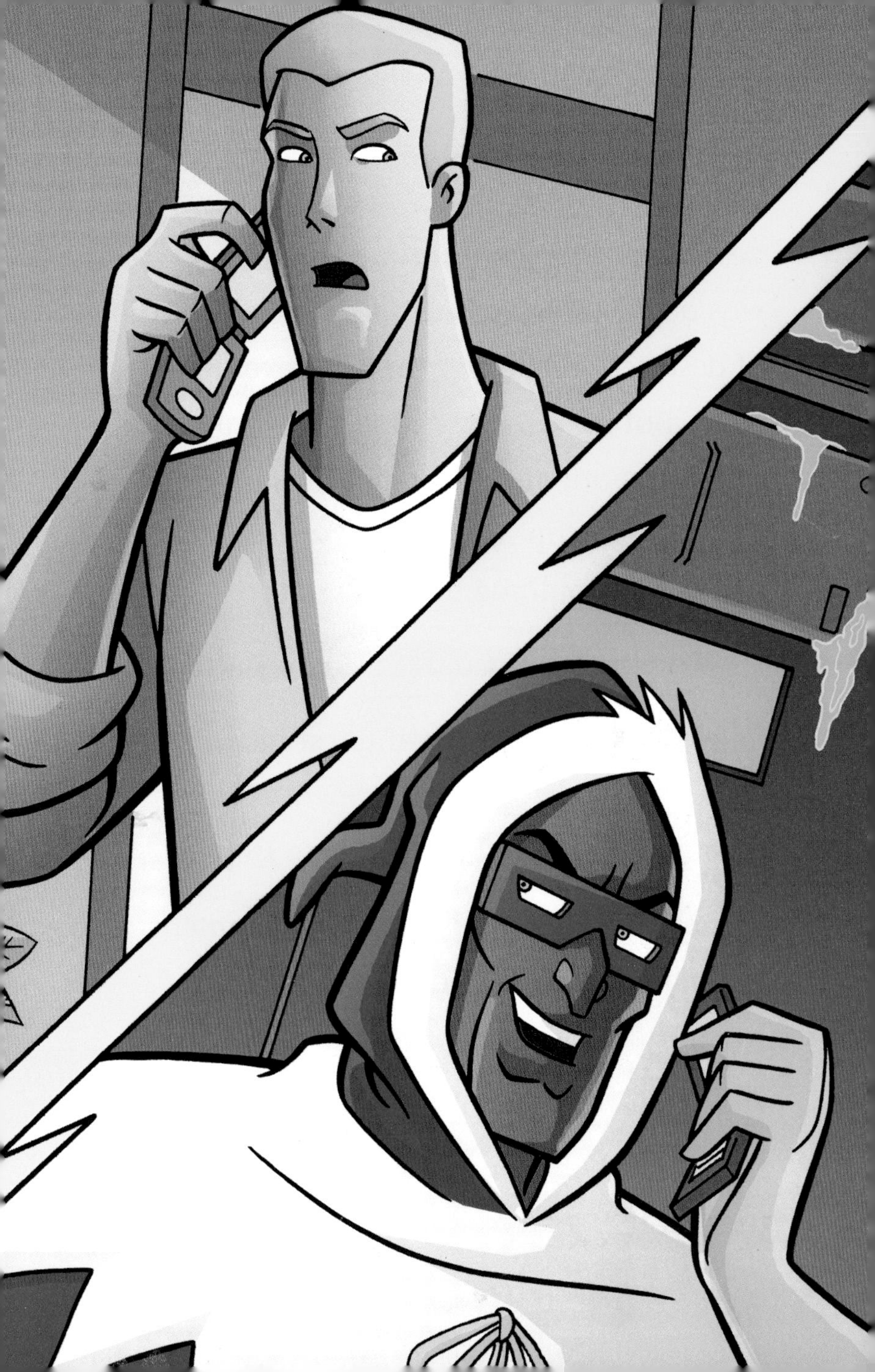

Flash knew that Captain Cold wouldn't care about the volcano, the island it would destroy, or the people who would die. Cold was a criminal mastermind who left a trail of destruction behind him wherever he went. But his ego was huge. He would care about the attention he'd get for stopping the biggest eruption in history. The challenge would be hard to refuse.

"The biggest?" Captain Cold asked.

Flash could hear the interest in his voice. "Yes," the super hero confirmed. "The biggest. And I need your help to stop it."

Captain Cold was silent for a moment. "Come to my laboratory, and we'll talk," he said. "But make it quick, or I just might change my mind."

Barry Allen hung up the phone and pressed the golden ring on his finger.

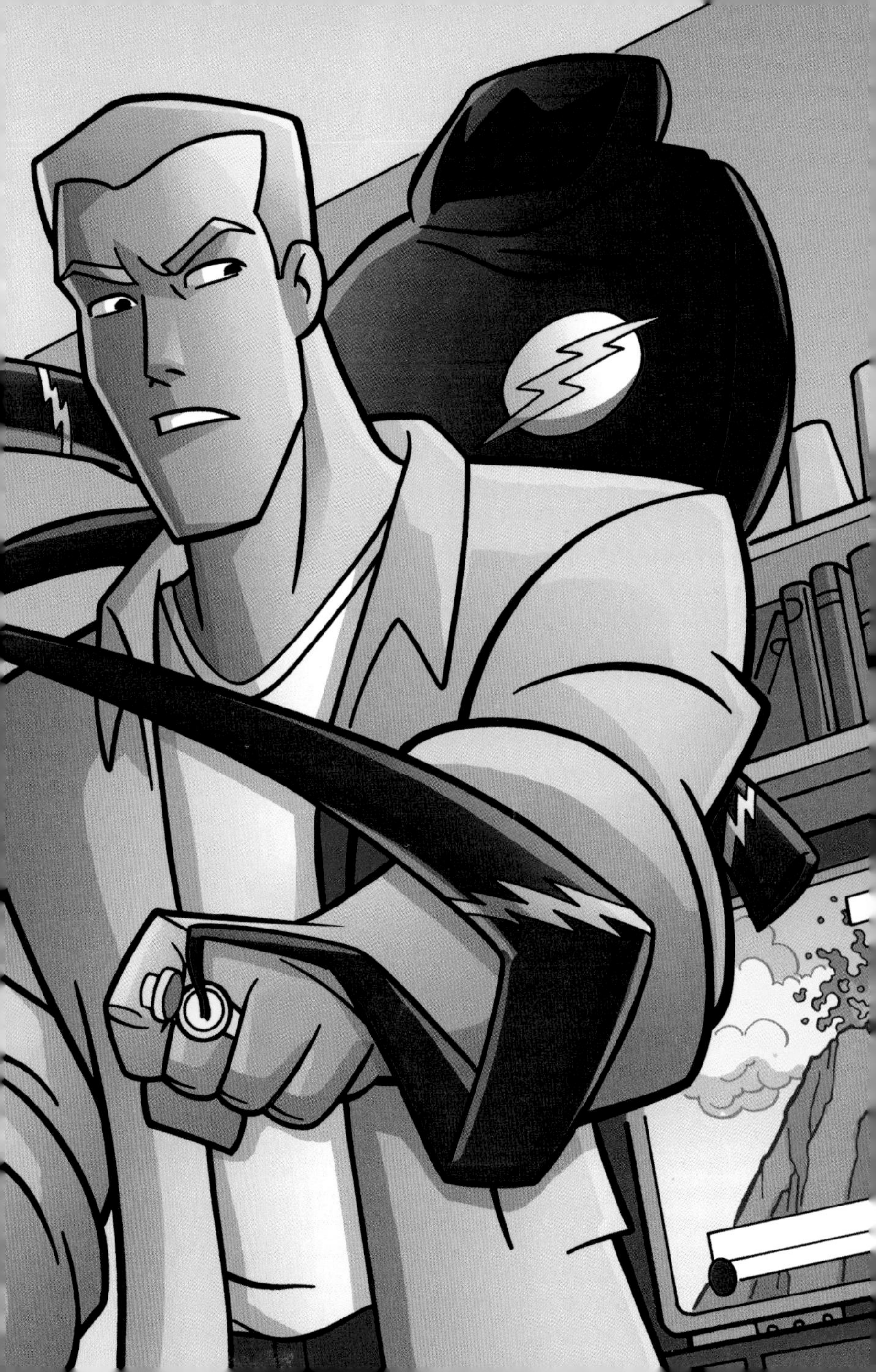

KLIKKK!

A tiny square of folded fabric shot out from inside the high-tech jewelry. As soon as it hit the air, the fabric began to expand. Seconds later, it was a life-sized uniform. The super hero slipped inside at super-speed, and the transformation was complete.

CUTTING A DEAL

ZWWWOOOOMMMM!

The Flash raced through Central City, a crimson streak of light against the dark night. Citizens heard the quiet roar as he sped by. They felt a warm breeze from his lightning-fast vibrations. But all they saw was a blazing trail of red and gold.

The Flash zoomed past apartment buildings, department stores, corner shops, and neighborhoods. He sped past them all, making his way toward the empty lots on the edge of the river.

On the far side of a string of rundown warehouses, Flash screeched to a halt in front of a large, steel door.

The steel doors opened. "I hope this isn't a mistake," the Flash said to himself as he entered the villain's lab.

In the dark shadows, the Flash could just make out the shape of Captain Cold's hood and the barrel of his weapon. The super-crook was pointing his freeze gun right at him!

"*Move!*" said a voice in Flash's head. But the super hero remained still. Showing fear would only give Captain Cold the upper hand in their temporary partnership.

"Freeze!" Captain Cold said, laughing.

"Very funny," replied Flash.

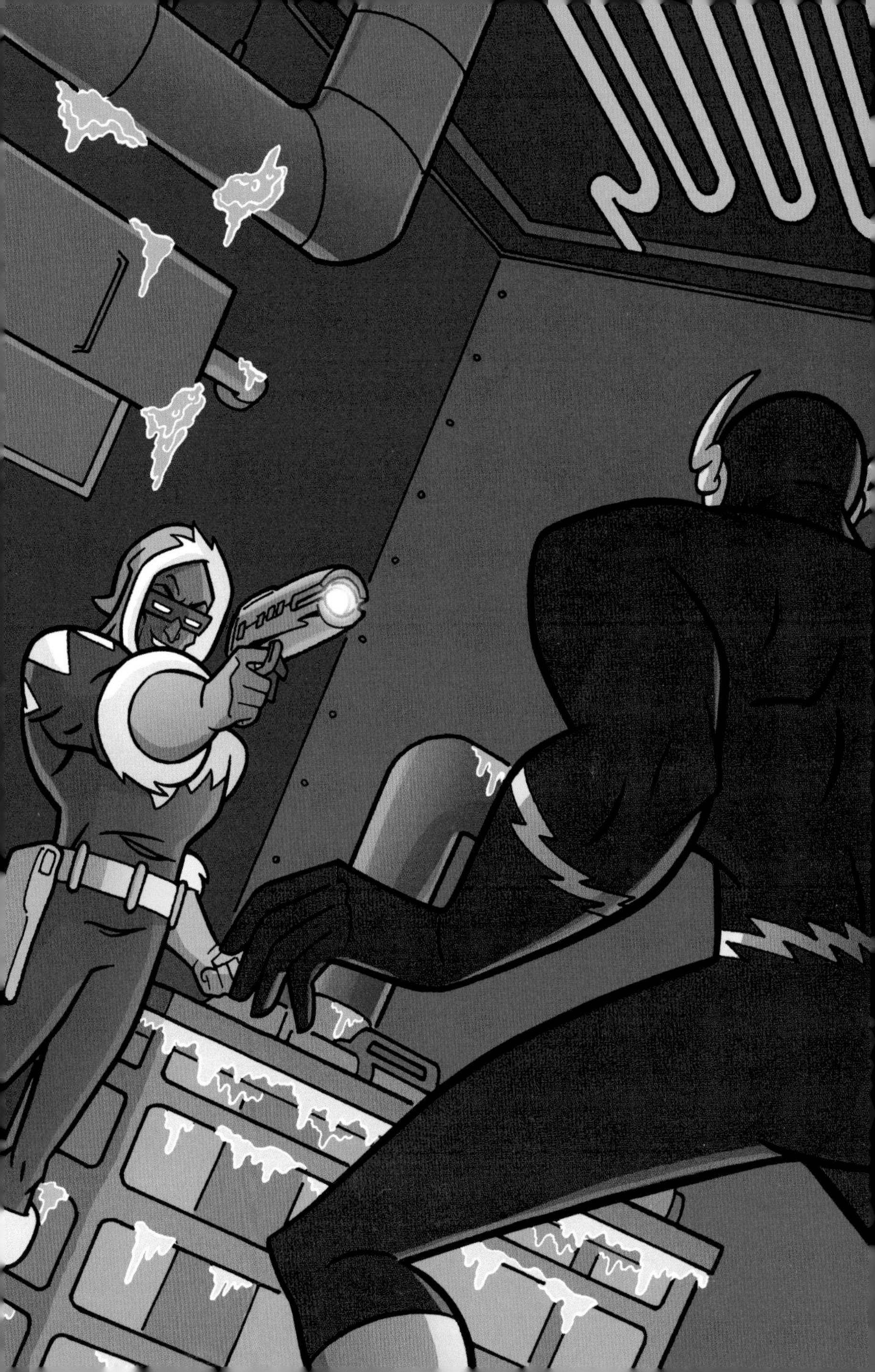

Captain Cold dropped the weapon to his side. "I thought so," he agreed. He held the door open wide and smiled wickedly. "That was quick, even for you."

Flash stepped further inside, ready to spring into super-speed at any second. He had never been to this hideout before. Caution was always wise in a new setting, especially when Captain Cold was nearby.

Dirty light bulbs on the ceiling lit up the warehouse laboratory. The Flash's eyes widened when he saw a collection of giant freeze guns on a nearby table.

"You're not the only one who follows the news, Flash," Captain Cold said. "I know all about the eruption of Mount Lavalo. But you're forgetting something — I'm not in the business of stopping catastrophes."

The Flash knew that Captain Cold wouldn't stop the eruption because it was the right thing to do. The chance to face his greatest challenge might not be enough motivation, either. The villain would need a stronger reason, such as fame or fortune.

"The island of Wiji would be forever in your debt," the Flash began. "They might even offer a handsome reward."

Captain Cold's eyes gleamed behind his radio-receiver glasses. "Do I have your word that you'll help me get the credit I deserve?" he asked.

"You have my word," the Flash said.

"You're such a goody-goody," said Captain Cold. "The task isn't difficult, really — at least not for a brilliant mastermind like me."

The Flash ignored Captain Cold's words. He looked past the villain to the machinery and freeze guns sitting on the table.

"Impressive, aren't they?" the villain asked. "It just so happens that your timing is excellent. I've been working on some new technology that has even more freezing power! Your little eruption gives me the perfect opportunity to test it out."

"It's not my eruption, Cold," the Flash corrected. "It's Mother Nature's."

Captain Cold packed several freeze guns into a special, weatherproof bag. "Mother Nature has nothing on Old Man Winter," he said with a laugh.

HAHAHAHA!

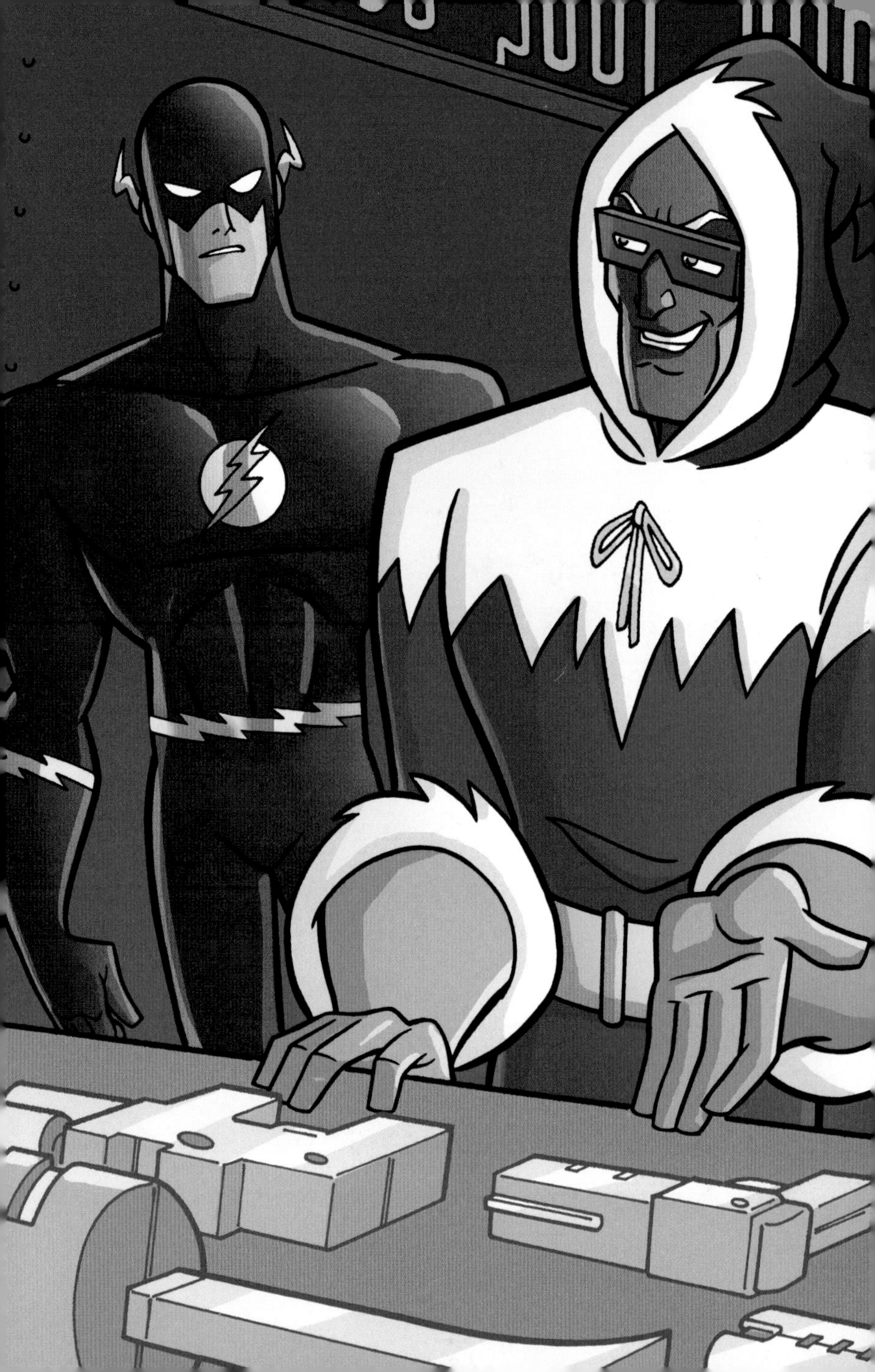

EARTHQUAKE!

BZZT! A few hours later, Captain Cold stood atop the giant volcano, firing a freeze gun down into its throat. With his special glasses, the super-villain could see far into the crater, but not as far as the magma chamber. Every minute or two, when Cold felt another powerful blast, he fired again. **BZZT!**

"I could help if you'd lend me a cold gun," the Flash said. He wasn't eager to use one of the weapons. As a rule, the Flash was weapon-free.

But the speedy super hero felt foolish just standing around doing nothing.

"Are you sure you could handle it?" Captain Cold began to say.

RUMMMMMMMMBLE! Suddenly, Mount Lavalo began to shake. It rocked slowly at first and then shuddered violently.

"Earthquake!" shouted Flash.

CRAAAAACK! A gaping hole opened in the ground nearby. Trees uprooted and crashed to the ground. A giant boulder near the top of the volcano broke free and started to roll down the mountain. The Flash whirled into action, racing down the steep, rocky slope. **WHOOOOSH!**

Not far below, the Flash could see a group of people scrambling for cover on the path.

One of them was carrying a TV camera. *Probably a crew on their way up to document the volcano,* Flash thought. He sped up and leaped over the boulder easily, but he still had to stop it. The massive rock was heading right toward the crew.

"Look out below!" the Scarlet Speedster warned. They couldn't hear him over the roar of the earthquake.

THUD! THUD! THUD!

The giant rock thundered down the mountain. **SMASH!** It crashed into a fallen tree, crunched through part of the trunk, and kept on going.

Flash moved so fast he was nothing but a blur, racing farther and farther in front of the rock. Then suddenly, he turned around and headed straight toward it.

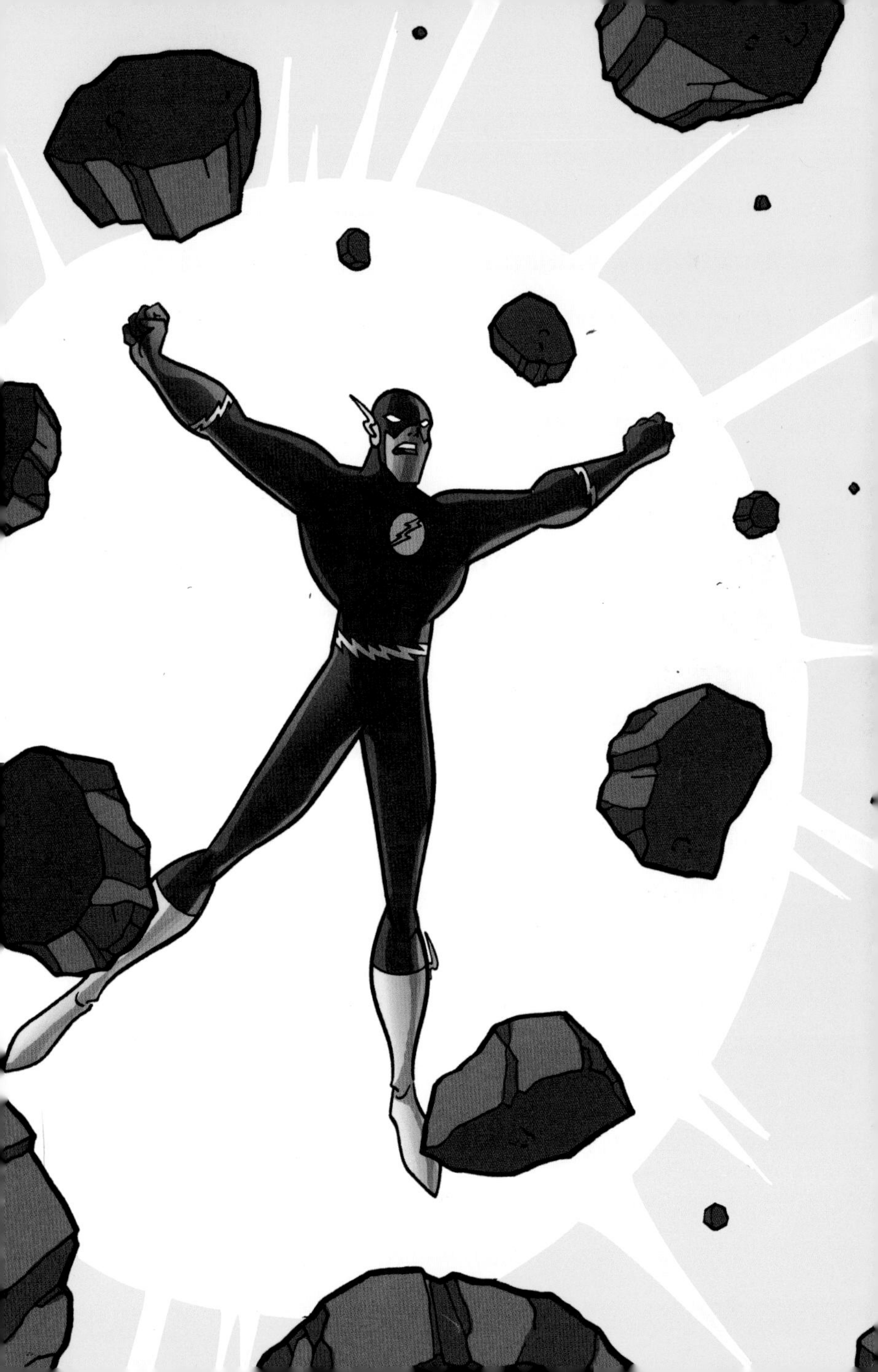

Moving faster than the speed of light, he vibrated right into the center of the tumbling boulder. He spun dizzily for a moment, and then he began to pulsate with all his strength.

KA-POW! The giant rock shattered into a thousand pieces. Several chunks landed at the feet of the reporters, who stared at the Flash in shock.

"Thank you!" the man holding the TV camera said as the ground became still.

"No problem," the Flash said.

Meanwhile, Captain Cold kept firing his cold gun into the volcano. The villain mopped his brow. "It's way too hot up here!" he shouted. "If I'd have known how much heat I'd have to take stopping this thing, I would've stayed home!"

The earth had stopped rumbling, and Captain Cold looked around at the tropical island. From the top of Mount Lavalo he could see almost everything — sparkling sea, sandy beaches, and green trees. It was pretty, he had to admit, but it was also hot. And Captain Cold hated the heat.

Captain Cold untied his hood and pulled it off. A light breeze ruffled his dark hair. *That's better,* he thought.

The villain felt a bead of sweat snake down his back. "I hate hot!" he shouted. "I despise tropical!" He fired the cold gun at the left side of the summit. **BLITT!**

Instantly, a whole patch of tropical island was frozen solid. **BLITT!** He fired it on the right, creating another frosty patch. Ice spread out in front of him.

BLITT! BLITT! BLITT!

A slow smile spread across his face as he pulled his hood back up. He looked around and laughed crazily.

Captain Cold had a new plan.

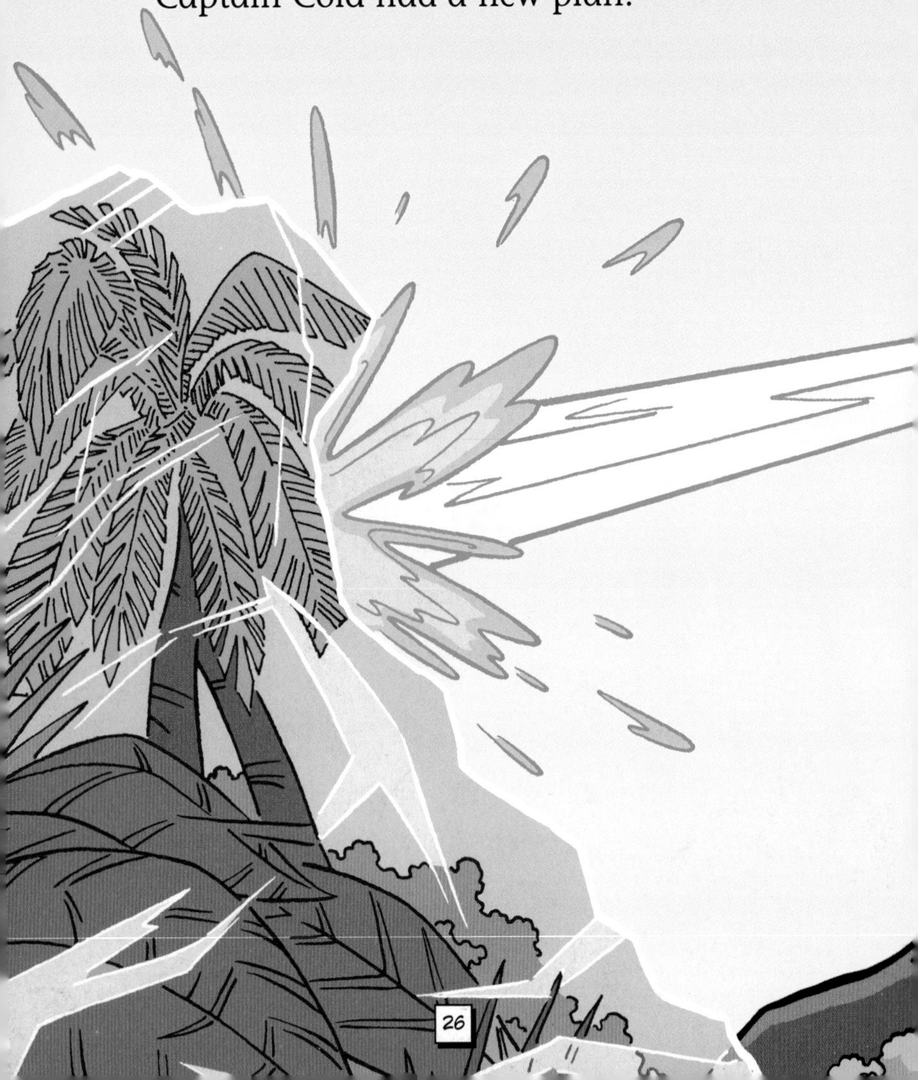

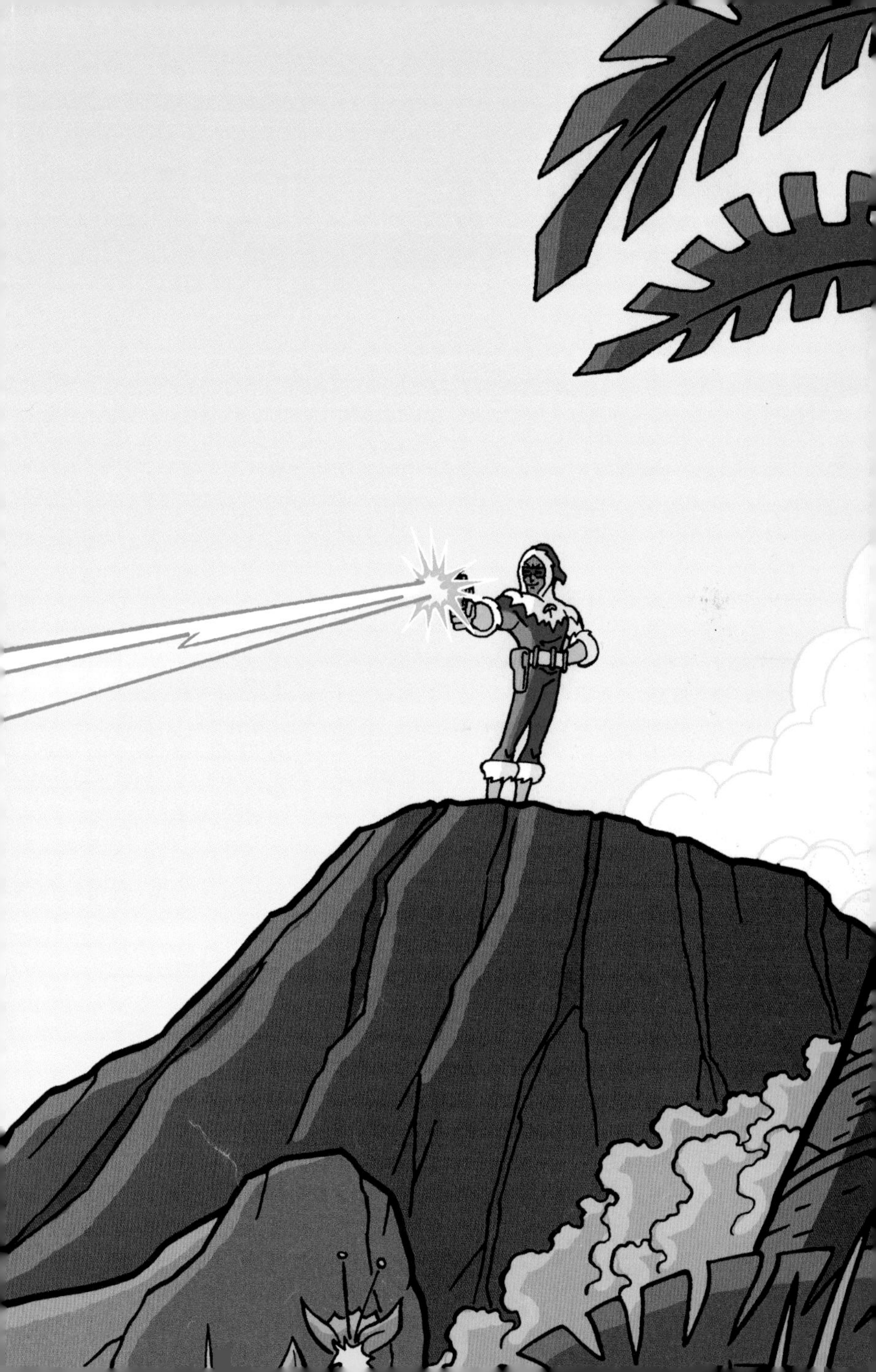

COLD SNAP!

At the base of the volcano, Flash felt a strange chill and looked around, confused. The average temperature on the island was 87 degrees. So why did he just shiver?

Looking up, he shivered again. This time it wasn't the air that chilled him. It was the sight of frozen palm trees. Entire sections of the top of Mount Lavalo were frozen solid with ice!

"That dirty crook!" Flash said under his breath. "Captain Cold's up to no good."

"What did you say?" one of the nearby reporters asked.

The Scarlet Speedster's face turned as red as his uniform. "Um, nothing," he replied. "I have to go!" He sped up the mountain like a race car.

WHOOOOSH!

"I should have known Captain Cold couldn't be trusted!" the Flash scolded himself. "It was stupid to leave him alone up there!"

The higher the Flash climbed, the cooler the air became. Luckily, the super hero's vibrations created their own heat and kept him from getting cold. The ground was slippery in places. Snow and ice slowed him down. He had to be very careful not to slip and fall.

When he reached the summit, Flash saw Captain Cold firing his freeze gun at everything in sight.

"What are you doing?!" the Flash shouted.

"What does it look like?" Captain Cold replied. "I'm cooling the place off. You said I had to stop the eruption. Well, I'm stopping it. And while I'm at it, I thought I'd give this island a much needed cold snap." The villain threw his head back and laughed. "I always wanted my own personal tundra!"

Captain Cold pointed his freeze gun at a hibiscus tree covered in beautiful pink blossoms and fired. *BZZT!* A second later, the entire plant was frozen. The flowers fell to the icy ground and shattered.

"You won't get any gratitude from the island residents if you destroy their beautiful nation!" the Flash said. "They'll hate you!"

HAHAHAHA! Captain Cold roared. "You just don't get it, do you, Flash?" he said. "Why would I give a hoot about their petty little gratitude when I can claim my own frozen island?"

The Flash felt foolish for trying to reason with the icy evildoer. How many times would he make that mistake? *Probably a hundred,* the super hero admitted to himself. The Flash always looked for the best in others — always wanted to give them the chance to show that they had some good inside.

Forget it, Flash told himself.

Whirling into action, Flash placed himself between Captain Cold and the section of jungle he was aiming at.

BZZZT! Captain Cold fired, and the Flash roared through the stream of ice. His vibrations were so fast that they created intense heat and melted the ice.

Captain Cold's face wrenched into a ball of fury. "You can't stop me!" he shrieked. "You don't have the power to stop me!"

The villain turned and fired again, but the Flash was ready.

VROOOOOM! He sped right into the stream of ice, melting it again.

"Arrrggggg!" Captain Cold bellowed. He turned to fire in another direction, but the same thing happened again. He'd never get his own personal tundra at this rate!

Captain Cold cracked a wicked smile. He aimed his freeze gun again. Only this time, he lowered the muzzle and fired at the ground beneath Flash's feet.

WHAM! Flash slipped and fell hard onto the ice.

"Oh, did that hurt?" Captain Cold said with a laugh. He raised his gun again and fired. **BZZZT!**

Flash tried to get up. The icy ground was so slippery he was running in place.

Captain Cold fired in every direction, aiming farther down the mountain. Flash saw the television crew in the distance, completely frozen.

He had to do something . . . and fast.

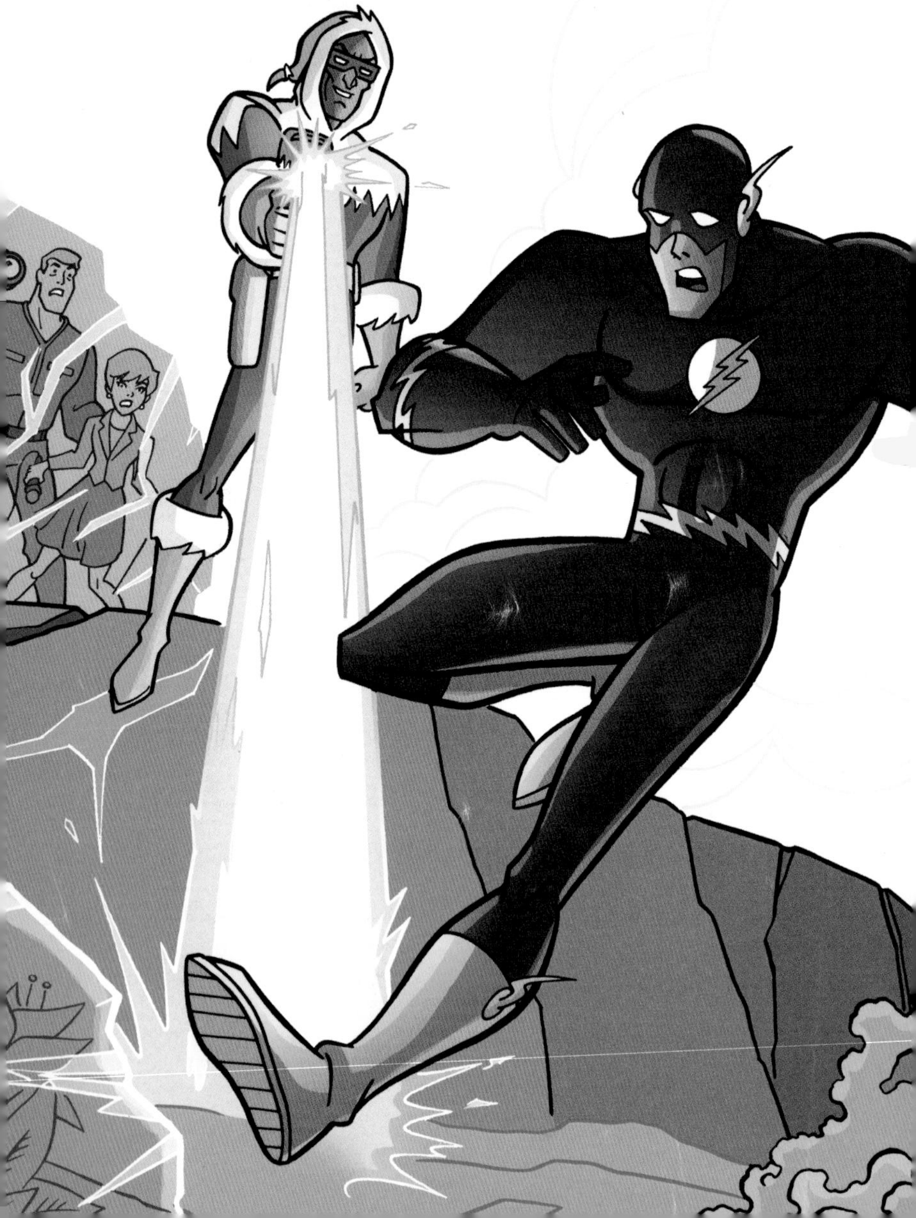

So, Flash ran. His boots moved up and down like pistons. After a minute, the ice under his feet began to melt. Soon he was standing in a puddle. Luckily, Captain Cold was having such a good time freezing everything in sight he didn't notice that Flash had melted the ice slick that had kept him running in place. The super hero had the advantage.

In an instant, the Flash became a streak of red. He raced in circles around Mount Lavalo, starting at the top and working his way down. He used all his superhuman strength to move as fast as he could. He left a path of vibrating warmth behind him, liquefying the snow wherever he went. Captain Cold's frozen island was suddenly having a warm spring day.

"You boy scout!" Captain Cold shouted. He tightened his grip on his ice gun. "You're no match for me!"

The villain ran to the area where he was storing his weapons and dashed inside. When Captain Cold reappeared, he was carrying the biggest, most powerful freeze gun the world had ever seen.

ZZZAPPPPPPP! He fired it down the side of Mount Lavalo, covering an entire square mile with solid ice.

"Take that!" he shouted.

Flash nearly fell on a newly formed patch of ice, but he managed to remain upright. The super hero screeched to a halt and looked around, grimly. With his new freeze gun, Captain Cold was even more powerful than before.

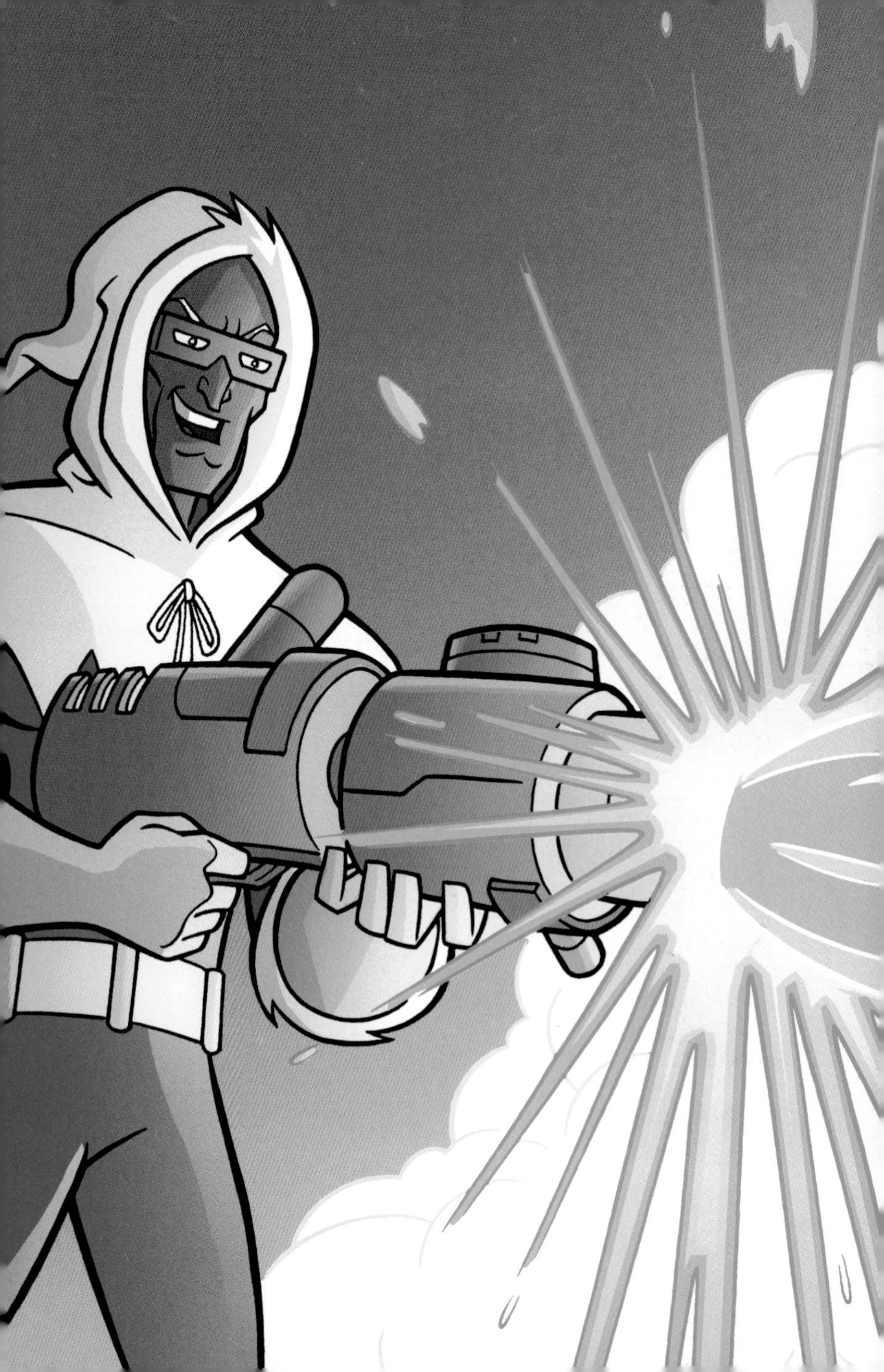

Being fast would not be enough to stop Captain Cold's spreading trail of ice. And the Flash was starting to run out of ideas.

SHOWDOWN

The giant freeze gun was firing so fast that Flash's head spun just watching the ice form. Furious, he charged at the evildoer. "That's enough!" the Flash shouted.

"I'm just getting started!" Captain Cold replied. He aimed the freeze gun at Flash.

The Fastest Man Alive darted aside so quickly that Captain Cold didn't see where he went. Guessing, he turned to his right and fired again.

A bubble of hot air came out of the top of the volcano like a burp. Flash raced up to the summit and peered into the throat. He was greeted by another gush of gas.

"Enough of this!" the Flash called to Captain Cold. "Hand me a gun! The chamber is heating up again. We need to cool it down, or we'll both die!"

ZZZAPPPPPPP! Captain Cold fired in a giant circle as he huffed his way up the volcano. "I'll handle it," the villain said, reaching the summit.

Captain Cold peered into the super-hot crater and was met by another steamy burst. He fired down the cone's throat, watching it freeze. "You see how easy it is to tame Mother Nature?" he boasted. "I'm a hundred times more powerful than she is!"

He fired into the air, and icy pellets rained down on the volcano. "A *thousand times* more powerful!"

Flash watched Captain Cold refreeze the areas he'd just thawed. The super hero began to understand just how crazy the villain had become. *I was foolish to think he would cooperate,* Flash thought.

"The volcano is going to erupt!" the Flash yelled. "Your job is to stop it."

"I'd rather stop you!" Captain Cold replied.

The villain aimed his weapon at Flash again. But this time, instead of dodging the blast of ice, Flash faced it head on. He stared down the barrel of the ice gun. He concentrated hard.

Like a volcano building up pressure beneath the surface, Flash boosted the energy inside of himself. The super hero recharged himself with speed until he was about to explode.

Captain Cold won't see this coming, he thought. Then, Flash erupted, blasting toward the villain's Freeze Ray. Moving too fast to be seen, the Scarlet Speedster disabled the weapon before the villain could even notice.

Captain Cold pulled the trigger. Nothing happened.

CLICK! CLICK! Captain Cold pulled the trigger over and over. Nothing.

"What have you done?!" Captain Cold screamed.

"Nothing much," the Flash said.

The super hero smiled and moved slowly toward the villain. Flash knew the weapon couldn't be used against him anymore.

CLICK! CLICK! Captain Cold tried again, but the gun would not fire.

In a rage, Captain Cold threw the useless gun aside and tackled Flash. The super hero was so surprised it took him half a second to realize what had happened — just enough time for Captain Cold to wrestle him to the ground.

Unfortunately for Captain Cold, the Flash didn't just run with blinding speed. He wrestled with blinding speed, too. In less than two seconds, Captain Cold was pinned.

Flash reached for the freeze gun the criminal mastermind had thrown aside.

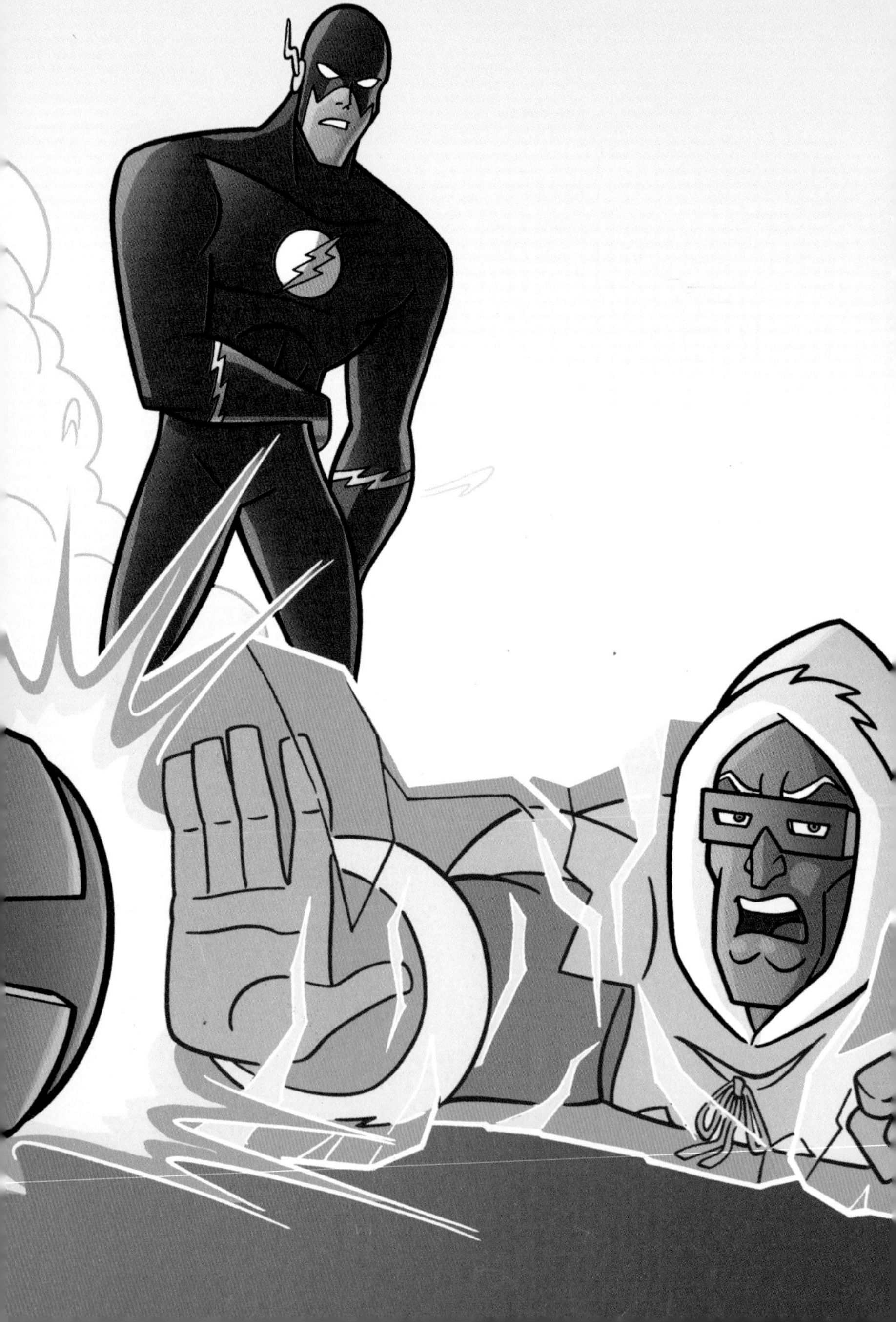

"Ooof!" Captain Cold elbowed the Flash in the side and tried to grab the gun.

BZZT! The gun accidentally fired, freezing Captain Cold!

"Your own personal tundra," the Flash said with a chuckle. "Looks like you got what you wanted after all." He thought he heard a squeaky sound come from the frozen figure.

"Don't worry," Flash told him. "You'll only be frozen long enough for me to get this volcano under control."

Flash carried the mega-freeze gun to the crater and fired several times down its throat. The rumbling in the volcano's belly stopped. The magma was cooling down.

All at once, Flash knew what to do.

The super hero collected several freeze guns and carefully put them in one of Captain Cold's bags. Then he sped down the volcano to the nearest science station. He handed the guns — and a quickly-written note explaining Captain Cold's plan — to the head geologist. He explained that these specially developed weapons could help stop the mega-eruption. Moments later, he was back at the top of Mount Lavalo.

"And now for you," the Flash said. He picked up the frozen shape that was Captain Cold and carried him to a recently formed lava lake, which was still partly churning and bubbling.

He deposited the villain right next to the hot lava and stood back to watch him thaw.

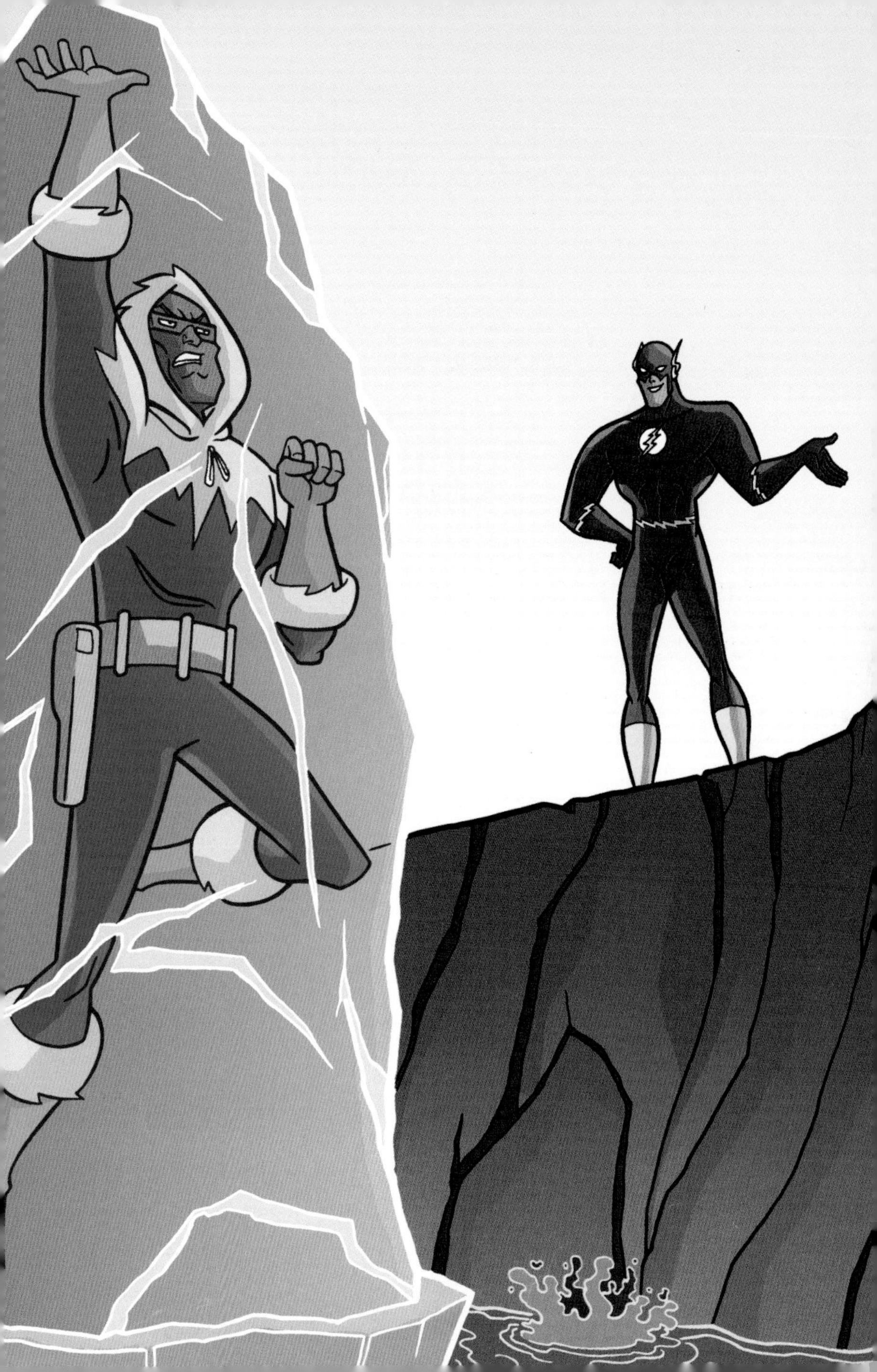

"I told you I wouldn't make you stay frozen for long," he chuckled. "Maybe now you'll chill out a little!"

* * *

Barry Allen smiled as he looked at the TV screen. It showed a warm, tropical landscape. The Pacific Ocean sparkled in the sun, and white-capped waves lapped on golden sands. Mount Lavalo, the biggest mountain on Wiji, stood tall against a clear blue sky. It was lovely to look at. And thanks to the Flash, Mount Lavalo was no longer a threat.

"Scientists are reporting that thanks to an amazing new technology in the form of an ice gun, they are able to control the temperature of the magma chamber deep in the heart of Mount Lavalo," said the news reporter.

"The threat of a mega-eruption has been snuffed out," the reporter said, smiling.

"In other news," continued the reporter, "the Flash alerted authorities to a man in a strange hooded outfit near the base of Mount Lavalo. The police recognized him as the criminal mastermind Captain Cold. The super-villain was quickly arrested for leaving his home state, a violation of his parole."

Barry knew that Captain Cold would be cooling off for a long while . . . in prison.

File Edit View Go Window Help

CAPTAIN COLD

done

CAPTAIN COLD

REAL NAME: LEONARD SNART

OCCUPATION: PROFESSIONAL CRIMINAL

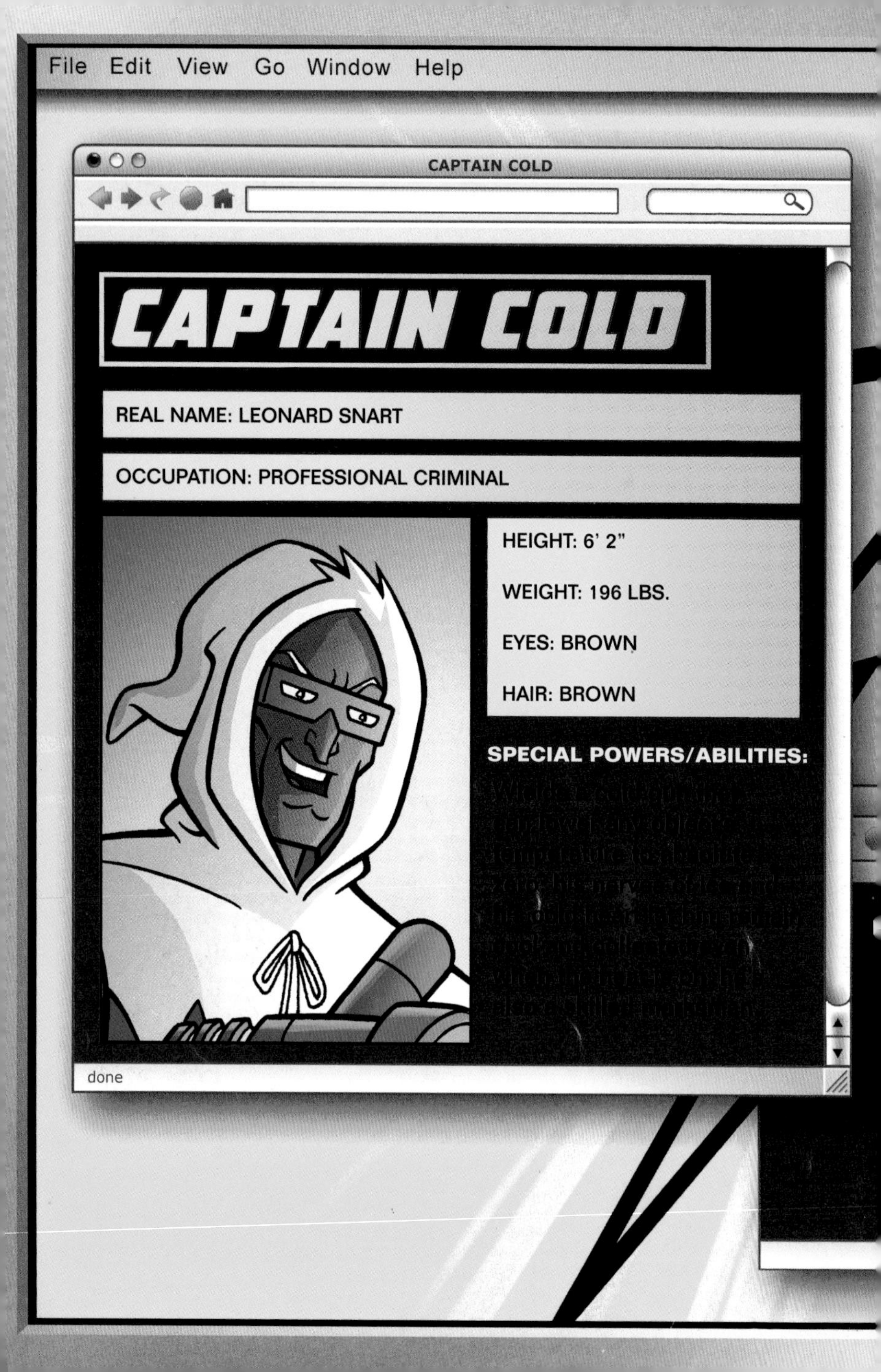

HEIGHT: 6' 2"

WEIGHT: 196 LBS.

EYES: BROWN

HAIR: BROWN

SPECIAL POWERS/ABILITIES:

[illegible]

Tue 6:23:12 PM Barry Allen

CAPTAIN COLD BIO

BIOGRAPHY:

Leonard Snart once terrorized Central City with a spree of cold-hearted crimes. No one could escape Captain Cold's icy grip — until the Flash showed up and put the super-villain on ice! Snart knew if he wanted to stay out of jail, he'd have to find a way to combat his super-speedy rival. So, he created an ultra-cold cannon that is capable of bringing even the Scarlet Speedster to a standstill! With the tide turned, Captain Cold looks to use this advantage to stop the Flash in his tracks.

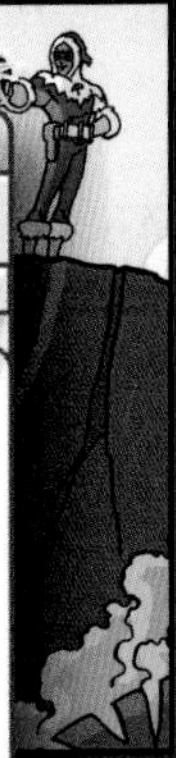

CAPTAIN COLD EXTRAS

Snart's snow goggles prevent him from being blinded by the ultra-bright flash of his cold guns.

The snow parka Snart wears keeps the cold out, protecting him from even sub-zero temperatures.

Captain Cold has ice grenades that can freeze everything in sight. Approach him with caution.

BIOGRAPHIES

Jane Mason is no super hero, but having three kids sometimes makes her wish she had superpowers. Jane has written children's books for more than fifteen years and hopes to continue doing so for fifty more. She makes her home in Oakland, California, with her husband, three children, their dog, and a gecko.

Dan Schoening was born in Victoria, B.C., Canada. From an early age, Dan has had a passion for animation and comic books. Currently, Dan does freelance work in the animation and game industry and spends a lot of time with his lovely little daughter, Paige.

Mike DeCarlo is a longtime contributor of comic art whose range extends from Batman and Iron Man to Bugs Bunny and Scooby-Doo. He resides in Connecticut with his wife and four children.

Lee Loughridge has been working in comics for more than fifteen years. He currently lives in sunny California in a tent on the beach.

GLOSSARY

catastrophe (kuh-TASS-truh-fee)—a terrible and sudden disaster

geologist (gee-OL-uh-jist)—someone who studies the earth's layers of soil and rock

lava (LAH-vuh)—the hot, liquid rock that pours out of a volcano when it erupts

magma (MAG-muh)—melted rock found beneath the earth's surface

mega-eruption (MEG-uh i-RUHPT-shuhn)—a large volcanic blast, capable of destroying all life on Earth

molten (MOHLT-uhn)—melted by heat

parole (puh-ROLE)—the early release of a prisoner, usually for good behavior

summit (SUHM-it)—the highest point, such as the summit of a mountain

tundra (TUHN-druh)—a cold area where there are no trees and the soil under the ground is permanently frozen

DISCUSSION QUESTIONS

1. Captain Cold is the Flash's archenemy. Why do you think the super hero chose to trust this villain? Did he make the right choice?

2. Do you think Captain Cold's punishment fits his crime? If so, why? If not, how would you have punished the super-villain differently?

3. Using his super-speed, the Flash can dash around the world in a split second. If you had super-speed, where in the world would you go? Why?

WRITING PROMPTS

1. Would you rather have the Flash's super-speed or Captain Cold's powerful cold guns? Write about the power you would choose and why.

2. Write another story where the Flash takes on Captain Cold. Where will they battle next time? Who will win? The choice is up to you.

3. Create your own super hero. First, write about your hero's abilities and powers. Will your hero have super-speed? Can he or she fly? Afterward, draw a picture of your crime fighter.

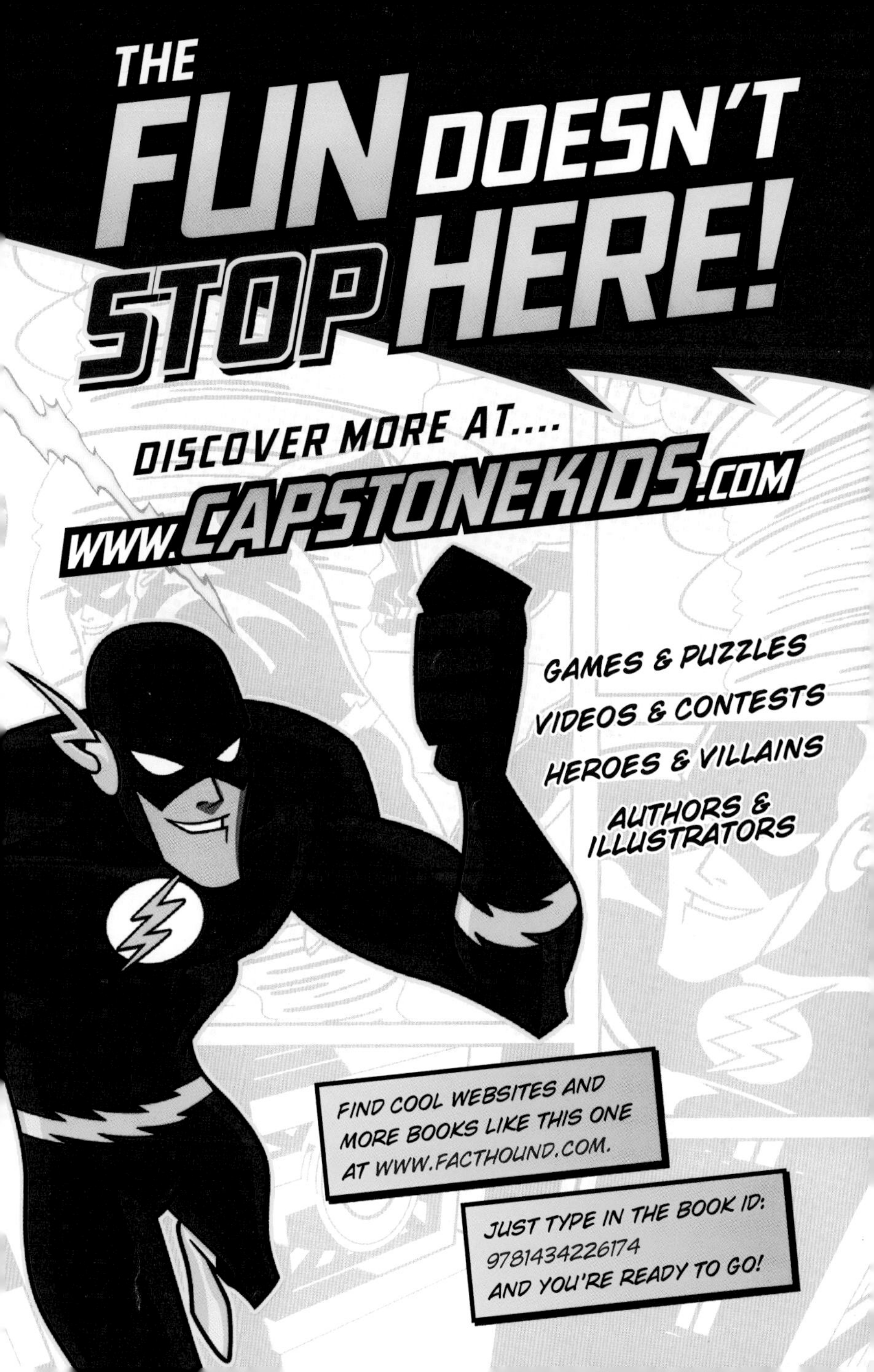
THE FUN DOESN'T STOP HERE!
DISCOVER MORE AT....
WWW.CAPSTONEKIDS.COM
GAMES & PUZZLES
VIDEOS & CONTESTS
HEROES & VILLAINS
AUTHORS & ILLUSTRATORS
FIND COOL WEBSITES AND MORE BOOKS LIKE THIS ONE AT WWW.FACTHOUND.COM.
JUST TYPE IN THE BOOK ID: 9781434226174 AND YOU'RE READY TO GO!

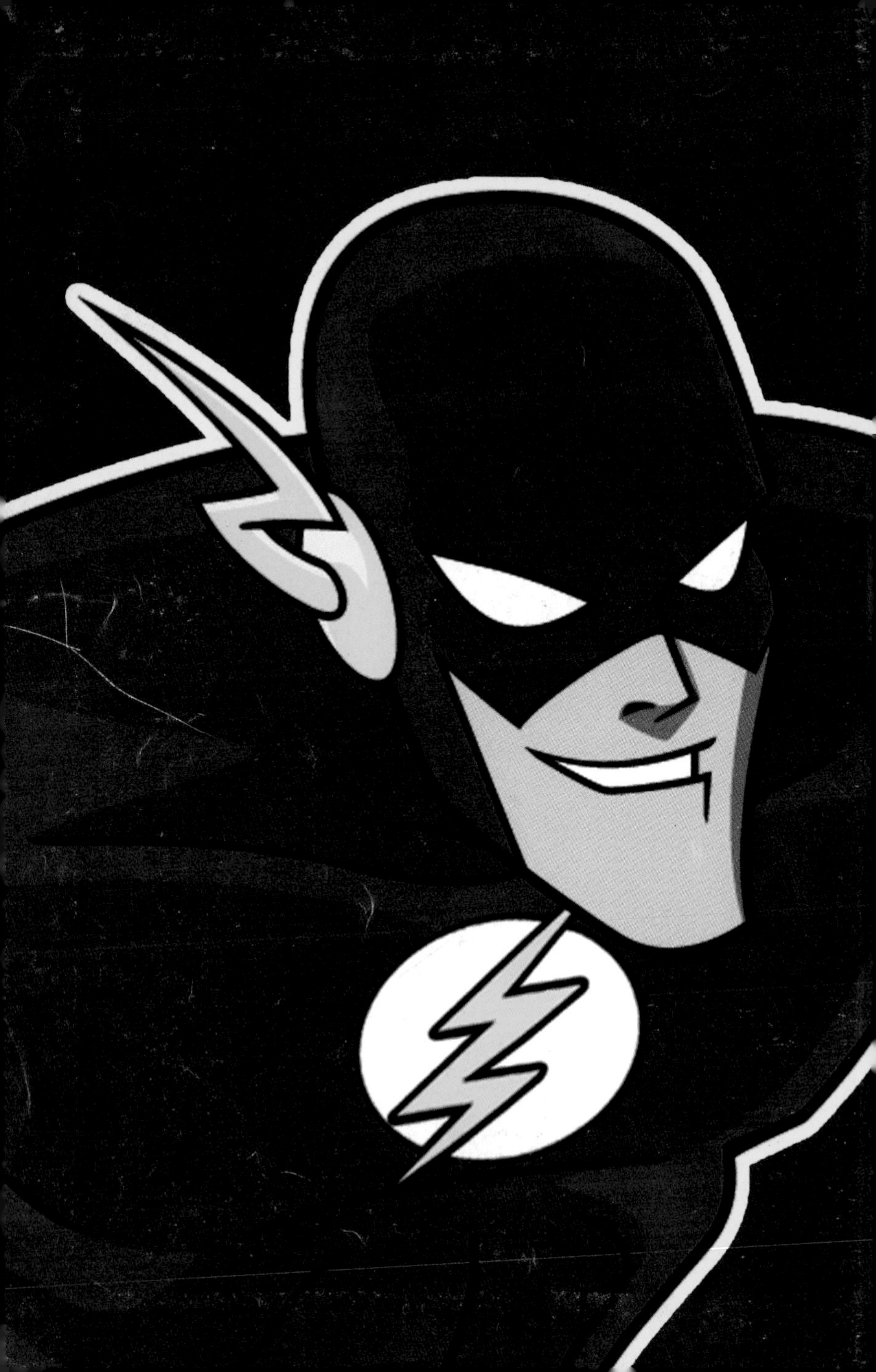